Beneath the Ocean
by J. N. Eagles

Hope you enjoy the story & always, keep the island in view!

— Jordan Eagle

Beneath the Ocean

Copyright © 2022 by J. N. Eagles

All rights reserved. No part of this book may be reproduced, stored in a retrieval system, or transmitted in any form or by any means—electronic, mechanical, photocopy, recording, or any other—except for brief quotations in printed reviews, without the prior written permission of the author.

This is a work of fiction. All characters are fictitious. People, events, incidents, descriptions, dialogue, and opinions expressed in this work are products of the author's imagination and are not to be construed as real.

First Edition March 2022
ISBN: 9798411174663

Cover designer: Jeanette Barroso
Illustrator: Elise Pullen

Other Works
by J. N. Eagles

Kings and Queens
A Beach for Us

To all those who are sailing or swimming,
land ho!

Contents

A Splash..9

The Seafarers..................................51

Scales..91

Part I
A Splash

Beneath the Ocean

Everything within me
kept shutting down.
In the undertow
of myself,
I felt like I was drowning.

J. N. Eagles

Everything around me
kept closing in.
In the undertow
of it all,
I felt like I was drowning.

Beneath the Ocean

Not until a mirror was found
tangled within my fishing net
did we understand riches existed
in the middle of the ocean.
Gems decorated the glass.
The golden handle weighed down
my hand, but the sailors took it,
carrying it away and concealing it from me.
They set our course for the island,
not realizing how delicate
a reflection could be.

J. N. Eagles

That mirror, I had gazed upon its glass,
saw my face for a fleeting moment.
I didn't recognize my appearance,
smudges of dirt, sunburnt skin,
tired eyes, and thin unsmiling lips.
Could this mirror be the first of many treasures
which would bring our sailing to a halt?
Claiming the riches could end our eternal search,
finally, able to rejoice in our farewell to the ocean.

Beneath the Ocean

The island, about which we only heard whispers.
The riches there could deliver us home,
but that place was so far away. Not sure of the direction.
Not sure if I wanted to return there.
Only sure of the direction of the treasure island—out to sea.
The sailors would rather be lost and searching,
than simply lost like me.

J. N. Eagles

Once, we thought we saw
a silhouette on the horizon,
a long, lowly shadow that resembled
our vision of the treasure island.
Though we sailed toward it,
the waves kept us at bay.
Constantly, the sailors stared into the mirror,
but, just like the horizon,
they never saw what they desired.
Then one foggy morning, the island
disappeared, and still we sailed
not knowing if we'd glimpse the outline again.

Beneath the Ocean

It seemed like a lifetime
that the sailors and I searched for the island.
Supposedly, when we landed there,
we were to find a chest hidden
beneath a warm blanket of sand.
Buried just below the surface,
treasure waited for us to claim it.
It seemed like a lifetime
that we sailed across the oceans,
day and night and day and night and day and night,
but we never came closer to the island or its promises.

J. N. Eagles

Deep was the ocean, but my mind went deeper
Eerie were the trenches of my thoughts
Paradise didn't exist for me
Realized the island might never be in sight
End end end end end end—will it end?
Swallowed the ocean until not a drop was left
Swore to myself I wouldn't survive
I did.
Ocean proved me wrong, stayed a little longer
Never gave in to the monsters inside

Beneath the Ocean

Tossing my net onto the wooden deck,
I climbed the railing.
Wind whipped my hair,
tugging as if beckoning me to step off.
I turned to check if the crew watched.
But while one was busy at the wheel,
and the other tightening the sails,
the waves continued their reach for me,
quietly whispering that they'll catch me.

J. N. Eagles

I took a breath,
a deep, deep breath.
Not knowing if I would get another chance,
but knowing that this was a better chance
to find the island rather than sailing,
I closed my eyes and
jumped.

Beneath the Ocean

I would find the island

Shocking, icy water embraced me
Pivotal moment as my senses awakened
Like it was the first time that I've
Actually felt, and felt more in these few
Seconds than I had on the boat in years
How was I supposed to deal with this?

Beneath the Ocean

Here I was
for the other sailors to see.
Yet not one noticed
I drifted farther out to sea.

J. N. Eagles

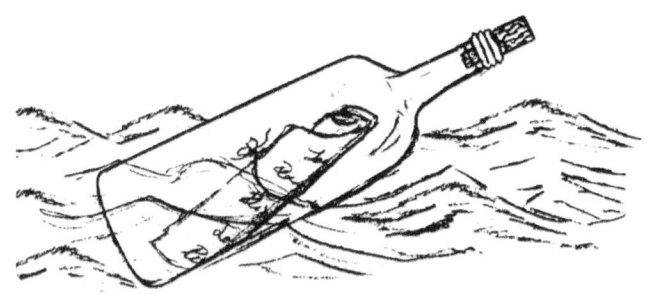

The current carried me.
I didn't know where I was,
wrenched farther from the boat.
How could the ocean be so sure?
For years, I sailed across the surface
and out of reach of its foaming fingers.
I thought being dry meant I was safe.
Was it possible the water tried to send a message?
Could it cleanse me, washing me all away?

Beneath the Ocean

Over and over
Confusion as
Each wave rolled,
Attacking me
Never allowing me to breathe

J. N. Eagles

Strange, to cry underwater
because you couldn't feel the tears,
but the burning of my cheeks still lingered.

Beneath the Ocean

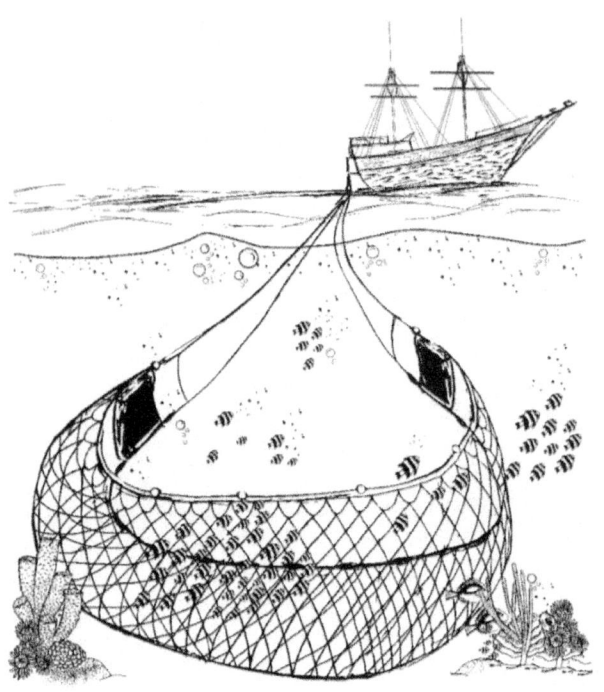

Living on the boat,
I never learned to swim.
We took what we caught,
so many fish our nets almost broke,
and threw the remnants back to sea
left to disappear in the depths.
Sinking farther,
the deeper I went,
the colder I became,
unable to fight the undercurrent.

J. N. Eagles

I had to dive
off the boat.
All the vessel did was deprive
me of feeling alive.
Two sailors
I left behind.
Who would find
the treasure island first?

Beneath the Ocean

The sun appeared
blurry and distorted
if you looked at it
from the bottom of the ocean.

J. N. Eagles

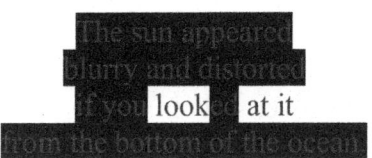

The sun appeared
blurry and distorted
if you looked at it
from the bottom of the ocean.

Beneath the Ocean

I struggled breathing air,
and I couldn't breathe in the water.
Never truly in control,
even on the wayward vessel,
we fought against the wind and current.
At the mercy of the fluid sea,
I was forced to face my fate.
It had to decide whether or not
to spit me out or let me rot.

J. N. Eagles

The next wave
could be my grave.
But maybe, just maybe
it could save
me.

Beneath the Ocean

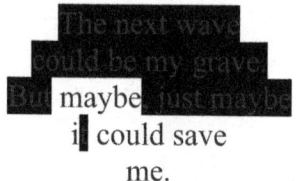
maybe, just maybe
i could save
me.

J. N. Eagles

The rocking motion made me seasick.
Pain and fear were the only emotions I could feel,
but the salt would help me heal.

Beneath the Ocean

I no longer saw the sails,
and didn't have a life vest,
but I needed something
to bring me to the surface.
On the boat, I rested too often.
Treading water, I grew weary.

J. N. Eagles

I ~~no longer saw the sails,~~
didn't ~~have a life vest~~
~~but I need~~ed ~~something~~
~~to bring me to the surface.~~
the boat ~~I rested too often.~~
~~Treading water, I grew weary.~~

Beneath the Ocean

Glittering within the deep,
they passed by and brushed against my leg.
I wanted to scream,
but water would've stifled the sound.
All around me, little fins flashed,
darting near and far, bumping
into my thigh, my knee, my feet.
The fish swam beneath me,
gifting me their scales.
They stuck to my legs until my waist
and below were covered with so many
that I couldn't see my skin.

J. N. Eagles

Finally, I reached the ocean floor,
so far away from the shore.
Still, the fish kept surrounding me.
I didn't feel anything, carefree.

Beneath the Ocean

Down, down, down
Running out of air in an
Ocean too deep to reach the surface
Walls of water everywhere
Nothing left for me, or so I thought
I stood on the bottom of the ocean
New me
Gone was the old. Reborn.

J. N. Eagles

```
                       here
                        I
                       was
           refused to be forced from
                       the
                      bottom
    of            the             ocean
     I         preferred         the
         silence    and    total
                    darkness
```

Beneath the Ocean

Here, it was dark enough
I couldn't see the monsters,
and cold enough
I became numb.
To stay meant to forget
all that happened above,
but leaving the ocean floor
would force me to confront
my reflection on the water's surface.

J. N. Eagles

I had to learn how to swim,
without once touching the water.
Us sailors always relied on the fishing ship.
If I were a different boater,
would the ocean still have accepted me?
Only one that jumped, I could have drowned yet,
the fish promised to guide me,
which the other deckhands had denied.

Beneath the Ocean

The boat never sailed
any closer to the island,
and the fish darted in many directions
as if not sure where to take me first.
Wherever it was that I belonged,
perhaps my tail could bring me there.
Perhaps it could take me to the sandy shores.

J. N. Eagles

I tied my long hair into a braid.
My blue and green scales glimmered.
All of me shimmered.
I had never felt more me
than when I was in this seafaring body.

Beneath the Ocean

I didn't understand,
had no idea why,
but the ocean kept me.
No need to be shy,
as my marine body was pretty
but not frail.
I belonged to the sea.

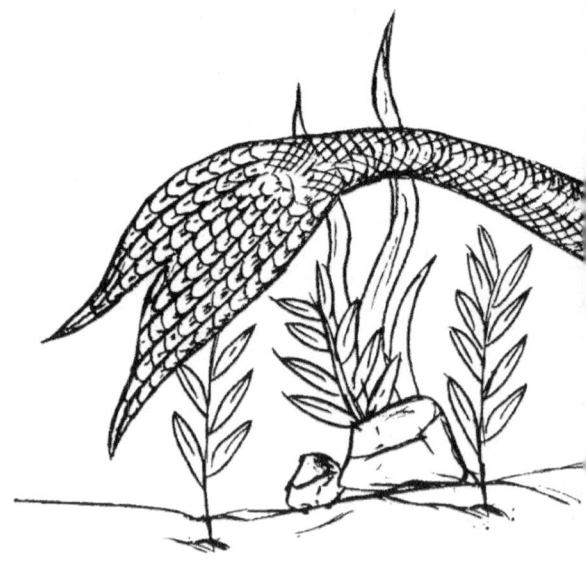

J. N. Eagles

Tightly, my feet concealed.
Another flick of my fin,
I thrusted forward faster than
Legs ever carried me.

Beneath the Ocean

Even with the water's fathomless weight
pressing, holding, and pulling my body,
I could still breathe.

J. N. Eagles

My blue-green scales shimmered
like a calm sea glittering in the
sunlight. Everything behind
me blinded. With each flip of my fin, I
soared forward, wondering if I could
swim faster than the boat could sail
without fear my tail would falter,
exhausted like my legs often were.
The slimy scales split the water
as if the ocean parted just so I
could swim through easily and
not have to stumble like I did
on the rocking boat, unsteady as
waves tried to overtake us and drown us.
Except it didn't want to keep us under. It
wanted to teach us how to swim with a
tail that looked like the sea.
That looked like me.

Beneath the Ocean

Water hugged me tightly
A friend who was always there
Vital for my survival
Existed to satisfy my thirst

J. N. Eagles

Surrounded by water but still thirsty
for more, felt like the boat had cursed me.
Though I jumped, I was still misplaced.
Water waved, and the boat's path erased.
To find where I belonged was my only wish.
Now there was no one to guide me but the fish.

Beneath the Ocean

The fish swam and I followed
right through a sea swallow.
The stormy waters weren't as rough
when I dove far enough
below the twilight zone.
Here, the ocean protected me as its own.

Part II
The Seafarers

Beneath the Ocean

I swam from school to school,
learning the ocean's history.
My mind swirled. A whirlpool.
Mermaids, trenches, and islands were a mystery.

J. N. Eagles

Agony—was I the only one?
Looked, still, for someone like me.
Outcasted by my shipmates. No other mermaids.
Needing another, despite the looming boat.
Except, that the ocean seemed empty of half-fish.

Beneath the Ocean

My troubles went deeper
than the water's surface.
Sometimes they blurred.
Didn't want the sea
monsters to wake.

J. N. Eagles

The fish must have sensed my fears.
They led me to a coral reef, where the warm
waters rocked me gently
back and forth.
The sea life welcomed me,
even the bubbles popping in my ear
were a blissful melody.
The seaweed, a soft bed for me to rest on.
If I could, I'd stay here for eternity.

Beneath the Ocean

Never saw another like me.
I stopped looking and dwelled
where I felt most free—the reef.
Unparalleled, only in this place
was a mermaid to feel relief.
Spreading my arms,
I embraced the next current.

J. N. Eagles

The treasure was so far from my mind.
The pressure to find it, to claim it
almost completely erased
by the gentle lapping of the tide.

Beneath the Ocean

almost

58

J. N. Eagles

Mermaid looking back at me
Inside the glass, the edges bejeweled
Right into my hands, the mirror sank
Right onto my path, the ocean
Opened up to me. I needed to keep searching
Realizing this, I lifted my chin toward the surface

Beneath the Ocean

A shadow overhead,
utopia shaded in gloom.
I spotted the underside of a boat.
Why did it have to obscure my sun?
Though innocently it seemed to float,
the reef dissolved into muted waters.

J. N. Eagles

Sun rose across the water
Around and around
If not found today, maybe tomorrow
Living on the boat for years
Ocean hadn't shown them its secret island
Refused to quit, sailors searched even when the
Sun sank beneath the water

Beneath the Ocean

The boat should have sunk long ago.
Many things weighed it down.
Yet, despite how heavy, still it floated.
Water held the craft high as if to keep the sailors dry.
Gently, waves caressed the wooden flanks,
asking the sailors for permission to reveal its secrets.

J. N. Eagles

A slow stop during their search.
Nothing in view—no island nor other boats.
Cursing abovedeck. Perhaps they're lost, too.
Help would not come until invited.
One day, they'll learn to help themselves—
Raise anchor and keep sailing.

Beneath the Ocean

Their anchor raked through coral.
Decades it took to grow.
In a moment, it lost its poise.
Crushed potential was immoral.
How I wished the sailors would just go.
None of us knew how ignorance could destroy.

J. N. Eagles

They hadn't changed
since I abandoned ship.
Still, the sailors interrupted
the life beneath them,
breaking coral and snaring fish.
I used to help them.
Now, I will swim next to the boat
and confront them,
revealing their reflection in the mirror.

Beneath the Ocean

Far into their journey,
Ideas of doubt started to form.
Should they keep searching?
Have they anything to lose? Nothing.
Involving other sailors or perhaps the fish,
Navigating could be easier with more eyes.
Glowing stars, unsure which to follow
Neither could deny uncertainty, so they
Each cast their boat's net.
They waited to see what it might catch.

J. N. Eagles

I was caught in the fishing net.
The sailors were a threat.
I couldn't cut the rope,
ran out of hope.
Slowly grew more tangled,
their desires left me strangled.

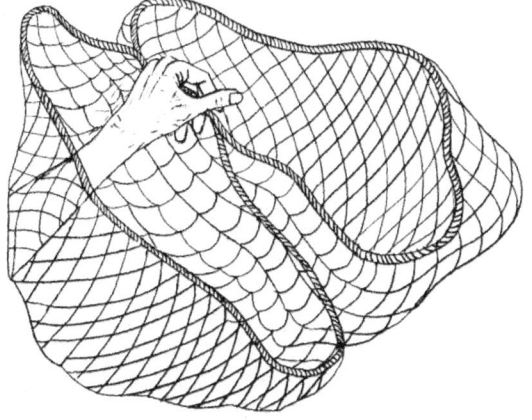

Beneath the Ocean

I had shared their boat. Did they recall?
Hunted for the island and floated above the waves.
Too busy fighting the sails to realize I had dove
into the clear seas. Now, too busy gazing
at my scales to see my face.
Trapped in the same net I used to throw out.
They didn't see me as an equal. I couldn't even speak,
gasping for water so my tail wouldn't dry.
Did they want me to suffer the same fate
as all the fish we used to catch?

J. N. Eagles

Sails
of white
were supposed
t
o
b
e
s
a
f
e
vessels, floating for those who couldn't swim, saving them
from the water. We were taught to fear drowning—it
should have been breathing. Twice now, I've
seen this vessel, and twice now, it should
have been peaceful.

Beneath the Ocean

Mistakenly, they thought
the boat would save them
and bring them to the island,
but it was never any nearer.
Mistakenly, they thought
the boat was safe to travel,
but it disrupted all the life
beneath the ocean.
Once I realized this, the ocean
took me in and changed me.

J. N. Eagles

Now that I was different,
They didn't want me to leave.
Flattered that they needed me,
but I couldn't show them the island when I
wasn't confident enough to walk across its sand
and still searched between the waves.

Beneath the Ocean

The sailors thought
they caught
a mermaid,
but they
really
caught a girl
who didn't
really
know who she was.

J. N. Eagles

How could I convince them
that I meant no harm?
How could I convince them
to release me when
it was my transformation that
they half-feared and
half-admired?

Beneath the Ocean

I wanted to scream, but instead,
I presented them the mirror,
the one I initially found, the one they discarded.
The sailors paused, shocked I saved it from the depths.
As one glared at their own reflection,
the other wrenched it from me
and returned it to their pocket.
They claimed they needed me *and* the treasure
so that they could finally stop sailing.

J. N. Eagles

They'd never tried,
so how would they understand
what the current could show them?
Instead, it was much easier to dismiss.
Delusions were necessary to uphold their pride.

Beneath the Ocean

The crew glared at me
with fishing hooks in hand.
Though they didn't even recognize
that behind all this mutation,
I was the sailor who shared their boat.
I had grown closer to the blue-green sea.
Jealous, they wanted to keep my scales
and throw overboard the rest of me.
Near enough that I could smell their breath,
they peeled a few scales off my tail
and tied them to rope to wear as proof.

J. N. Eagles

In the
ocean, passing the ship, was
a whale who heard my cries and swam
to aid. Once again, the ocean saved me. Saw me in peril
and created a tidal wave with its massive tail in order
to free me from the sailors obsessed with my
mermaid-green apparel. The
marine life stripped wood
from the ship as its
tail hit the water near
the vessel until the
boaters were in fear of
sinking and their future
rocked back and forth, unclear.

Beneath the Ocean

The sailors insisted
I needed their ship to thrive
but their ideals were twisted.
I was never more alive
than when I jumped into the water
and swam away from their lifeboat.

J. N. Eagles

The sailors ~~insisted~~
~~that~~ I needed ~~their ship~~ to ~~thrive,~~
~~but their ideals were twisted.~~
~~I had never been more alive~~
~~than when I~~ jump~~ed into the water~~
~~and swam away~~ from their ~~life~~boat.

Beneath the Ocean

Though the sailors were left
with a few of my scales
to tell their sea-worthy tale,
no one was there to listen to it.
From the time they caught me in their fishing net
to the moment the whale saved me,
they had not sailed any closer to the island.

J. N. Eagles

I'm glad there wasn't another mermaid.
Wouldn't want them to experience
the same thing with the sailors.
What would they have done had I not escaped?
Not made to stay in the open,
I would have dried out.
A terrible death for a fish.
Would they have stopped their search?
Perhaps they would have abandoned the island,
taking an innocent away from the shore.
Glad there wasn't another mermaid.
I never wanted them to feel betrayed.

Beneath the Ocean

When I left, I took refuge in the coral reef
where I would express my grief
for my missing mermaid scales.
Hidden between the rocks, an eel
warned me to keep fleeing the white sails
and promised that I would heal.

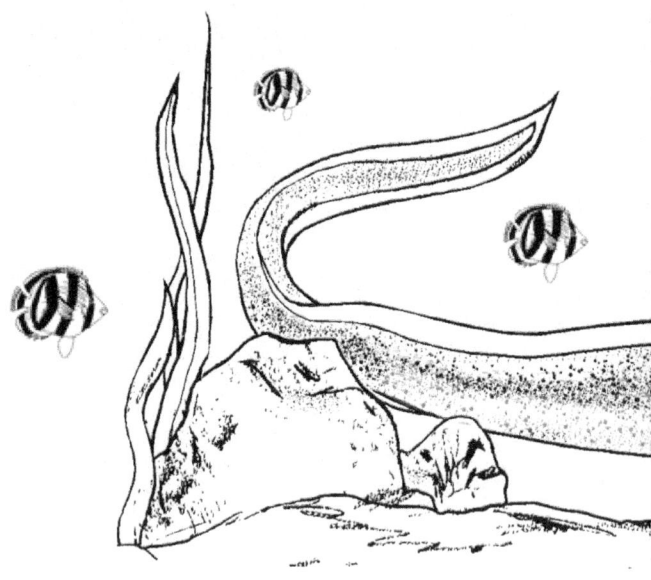

J. N. Eagles

When would I heal.

Beneath the Ocean

Would I see the white sails again?
Or was the island too hard to obtain?
Would I become entangled once again,
trapped in their trawler, a wooden pen?
I would have to escape once again.
Into the water, would they follow me then?

J. N. Eagles

I traveled across oceans with my tail
pushing me, while I ignored my emotions.
I hadn't seen the sailors
since they threw their net.
Were they still floating
on their wooden cages
or was the vessel slowly leaking?
The island they would always be seeking.

Beneath the Ocean

I traveled across oceans with my tail
pushing me, while I ignored my emotions.
hadn't seen the sailors
since they threw their net.
Were they still floating
on their wooden cages,
or was the vessel slowly leaking?
The island they would always be seeking.

J. N. Eagles

These mixed thoughts of blue and green
distracted me long enough that I lost
sight of the fish that had swam ahead of me.
I didn't recognize this part of the ocean,
yet the undercurrent kept pulling me
farther down, farther than I had ever been.
With dim sunlight, few fish and plants lived here,
but I managed to spot a hidden trench.
I would have kept swimming, except I thought
I caught sight of a fin and decided to swim in.

Beneath the Ocean

There was something dangerous
apart from the deepest ocean floor crack.
The water was so dark it seemed black.
The fear of it gripping me was monstrous.
Near the bottom, it would watch with two eyes,
and I knew anything that ventured down there dies.

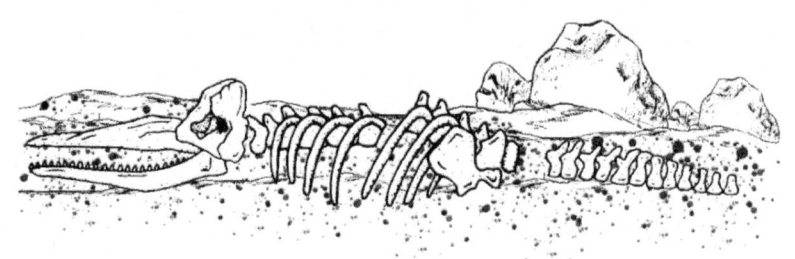

J. N. Eagles

part of me would die.

Part III
Scales

Beneath the Ocean

Instead of the treasure island,
my travels brought me to the deep cave.
What would I find within the shadows?
Didn't need to relapse back into the dark blue.
A lone fish beckoned me to follow,
and the ocean hadn't failed me yet.

J. N. Eagles

I swam inside
wasn't as dark as I thought.
Glowing seaweed grew from the sandy floor.
Too close, and my skin bubbled,
but the poisonous plant led me forward.
Focused on the cave, all fear and nerves, I forgot,
ignoring my unpleasant guide.
My legs. Nothing else I wanted more.

Beneath the Ocean

Scales shimmered even in murky water.
She smiled with shark-pointed teeth.
I should have swum away as fast as I could,
but, instead, I drifted closer.
It was more monster
than mermaid, and I understood how the sailors
half-admired and half-feared me.
She was what I could become.

J. N. Eagles

Mermaids were rare
with our ability to blend in,
except for the areas of exposed skin.
If they knew we existed, people might stare.
Never wonder what went on beneath the surface
when we're already halfway gone.

Beneath the Ocean

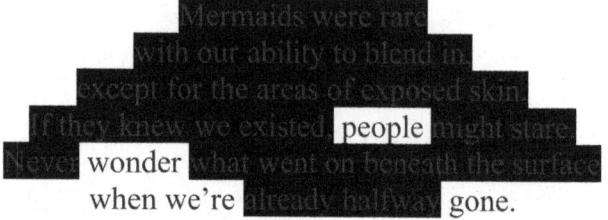

people
wonder
when we're gone.

J. N. Eagles

Hair floated in every direction.
The ocean showed me a reflection.
The mermaid even had a tail,
but the blue and green scales were pale.
Had she ever tried to leave,
or did the cave dweller not believe
that she could walk along the sand
and on two legs, bravely stand?

Beneath the Ocean

If I stayed there in the ocean,
would I become like this other mermaid?
More fish than human, gills frilled along her neck.
She didn't have to surface
to breathe in air.
With the poisonous, glowing seaweed,
she didn't have to surface
to see the sun.

J. N. Eagles

The warmth of a breeze,
she would never feel again
if she stayed here in the ocean.
She didn't know what she was missing,
and neither did I,
never having been to the island.

Beneath the Ocean

Cloudy waters distorted the scales
of the mermaid's blue and green tail.
Living in the sea for so long
caused her to be less than human.
Grinning, she beckoned me to stay.
I thought the ocean was a safe place,
but not all of it was a refuge.

J. N. Eagles

Trapped between two worlds,
the sea and above,
scales and skin, tail and lungs,
it was time for me to decide.
To save myself,
I had to leave the bottom of the ocean.

Beneath the Ocean

I felt something change inside.
My outward appearance reflected it.
Scales peeled and floated to the ocean floor.
My blue and green tail split in two,
legs revealed beneath the fin.
I had thought they were gone forever,
but this half of me that I believed was lost
finally returned. Newly formed.

J. N. Eagles

Me.
Even once called a myth, a fairy tale, I was
Real real real real real real
Me.
Alive alive alive alive alive alive
In this world, no matter who I was in the past.
Doing myself a favor, I swam toward the surface.

Beneath the Ocean

```
    t
 e    a
    k
```

                              a

```
    b   r
  h       e
    t   a
```

J. N. Eagles

Here I was again
Utterly astonished at the sea
Movement, the current's grasp released me
Altering directions, it led me across the surface
Needed poof that even with my legs, it was here

Beneath the Ocean

Legs weren't as alluring
as a mermaid's fin,
but they were more reassuring.
I had needed to accept my skin.
From my waist to the tip of what once was my tail,
such a waste, it hadn't made me whole.

J. N. Eagles

Sometimes we lost focus
and slipped beneath the waves.
The salt water, it could choke us.
It was not until we found a renewed purpose
that we managed to break the surface.

Beneath the Ocean

Salty ocean tears
pushed me into motion.
For so long I had floated,
never fully devoted,
living life on the shallow side
and drifting along the high tide
until the current changed course
and forced
me to hear the seagull's cries
and open my eyes.

J. N. Eagles

></p>
The wave
held my hand, intertwining
its white fingers in mine.
I was unsteady, but the water
waited patiently until I decided
whether I wanted to leave the
open ocean. It was so kind to me.
Can I still visit the shallows?
The water soothed my raging mind.
The ocean accepted me when no one else did.
I must take what I've learned and walk across the shore.

Beneath the Ocean

The shore, I longed for.
The ocean cleansed me
of the past.
I was ready for the water
droplets to dry in the sunlight.
Now that I was human again,
I had the chance to walk on the beach.

J. N. Eagles

The ocean pushed me out.
Its large waves shouted,
foaming at the edges.
I stood on the ledge,
the thinning beach
between sea and land.
There, I now could stand.

Beneath the Ocean

Standing on the edge, I was
Already dry from the sun.
Next to the blue-green water, but
Detached from the island no longer.

J. N. Eagles

My past,
when I sunk
and almost drowned,
I left it all at sea.

Beneath the Ocean

I didn't think anyone
would ever truly
know and understand
everything that went on
in the depths of the ocean.

J. N. Eagles

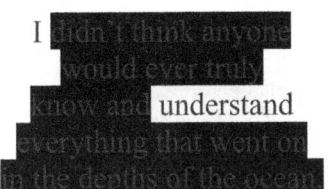
I understand

Beneath the Ocean

I didn't understand
had no idea why
but the ocean kept me.
No need to be shy,
as my marine body was pretty
but not frail
I belonged to the sea

J. N. Eagles

They'd never tried,
so how would they understand
what the current could show them?
Instead, it was much easier to dismiss.
Delusions were necessary to uphold their pride

Beneath the Ocean

My beautiful tail was never enough.
It couldn't carry me above the surface,
though it braved the roughest currents.
A keepsake I wanted, didn't want to dispose of
my blue and green scales completely.
I wouldn't mind saving a few discreetly.

J. N. Eagles

Sometimes, I miss my tail
and the blue and green scales.
Though the water was cold,
the current helped me feel bold.
I had felt at home in the coral reef,
but it was temporary relief.
Beneath the sea, I grew so much,
learning about myself as such.

Beneath the Ocean

Covered in sand, I spotted a thread
of mermaid scales
that were once part of my fin,
and I wondered if the sailors were dead.
Had the ocean finally swallowed their sails?
Tying the necklace, I wore it warm against my skin.

J. N. Eagles

Broken ship lay on the shore.
This was the place many tried to reach.
Different currents. Same destination.
The sand seeped warmth into my cold feet,
while the seagulls sang a welcoming song
I had never heard before.
The palm trees swayed in a gentle breeze
as if the branches were to embrace me on the beach.
I've struggled to gain my salvation,
but I'd never change what I endured to reach it.
The view is more beautiful because of it.

Beneath the Ocean

o
n
c
e
we were all on the same ship, living off the water
but not living in it and searching for
the island that would

save us from the depths of the ocean but it was the
ocean that
saved
us

J. N. Eagles

A beached vessel couldn't sink,
nor could it be lost on the sea.
After all they've been through,
almost sinking when the whale crashed
into the boat, losing everything,
and having to wade their way here,
they've finally made it to the island safely.

Beneath the Ocean

The sailors stood near their ship.
They were different, floundering on sea legs,
not as confident, as they scoured the shore.
Hesitating, not sure if they'd try to capture me.
Who would they remember me as—
The crewmate or the mermaid?
I avoided stepping in their sandy foot prints,
as they only searched for the treasure and
didn't notice how golden
the coast was beneath their feet.

J. N. Eagles

Two sailors dug along the beach,
Ruining the perfectly smooth shore
Each sand pile wiped away by the waves
Another area searched, only to find it empty
Soon, too quickly, they abandoned hope
Uncertain if the buried chest was there
Riches seemed out of reach once again
Eager to leave in pursuit of another island

Beneath the Ocean

The one who had worn my scales around their neck,
was upset about their beached ship, broken in two.
They took parts of the wood and parts of the island
and built a raft out of old pieces and palm trees.
The sailor traveled back to sea alone,
a mermaid on their mind.

J. N. Eagles

Here, there was no reason to write a sandy SOS.
Everyone was already saved.
Let's enjoy each other and solid ground.
Please, sailor, return to our sacred island.

Beneath the Ocean

```
                       One
                    started to
                   build a castle
                     out of
                      sand
                      and
        I            wondered if they will need a
      hand           or if this was the type of thing
   that needed      to be done by themselves, and
        I            would understand, of course, I
      went       from living a human life to being
```

half fish to being full human again. For each of us,
we had to build our own sandcastles and learn how much
water we needed to keep the parts together and how much
sand we needed to fit everything inside, and some had to
build far enough up the shore that waves didn't erode it when
they rolled up the beach. Regardless of how we developed it,
we had to turn the sand into our castles and into our homes.

There once
lived a rumor
of treasure
hidden on
the island.
There was.
It's us.

Beneath the Ocean

I never once dug in the sand.
There was no reason for me to search for treasure
when I had stopped sailing long ago.

J. N. Eagles

The sailor who stayed
saw me and waved.
I waved back,
as did the ocean.

Acknowledgments

Thank you to my family and friends. Especially, my little mermaid who inspires me every day, and my husband and my father for reading one of the first drafts. I love y'all. These poems wouldn't be here without everyone's love and support.

Thank you, Professor McCall, for your guidance and encouragement. You kept pushing me to write more and expand more. Though the project kept growing, many poems were cut or revised, in order to make this the best I could. This book wouldn't be the same without you.

Thank you to all the beta readers and editors who worked with me, especially under such a tight timeframe, to help improve and make these poems stronger. Revising can be a daunting process, but with y'all, it's much more enjoyable. Also, a special thank you to Jeanette and Elise for doing an amazing job on the cover and illustrations. Like *Kings and Queens*, your artwork brought this book to the next level. I hope we continue to work together.

Thank you, readers, for giving me the chance to entertain you with this fantasy tale. I hope your feet are always covered with sand.

About the Author

J. N. Eagles currently lives in Alabama with her husband and daughter, two cats, beta fish, and a flock of chickens. She runs a reading blog where she posts reviews about the books on her shelves, and she plans to write many books of poetry. She graduated from Athens State University with a Bachelor's in English/Language Arts and graduated from the University of North Alabama with a Master of Arts in Writing. When she's not reading or scribbling new stories, she's enjoying the outdoors and working in her garden.

Blog: https://life-on-the-shelf.com/

Instagram: @j.n.eagles.author

Facebook: @J. N. Eagles

Made in the USA
Columbia, SC
21 March 2022